Emily Dickinson

献给孤独心灵的礼物

全彩珍藏版

这世界，静默如初

下

[美]艾米莉·狄金森◎著

王晋华◎译

Selected Poems of
Emily Dickinson

台海出版社

目录 Contents

避世的冥想

孤独与喧嚣

目录 Contents

生与死的启示

目录
Contents

灵魂的自由

避世的冥想
Reclusive Meditation

就像新月（NO.1605）

已经失掉的，依然是我们身上的构成
那一部分仍然附着着，
就像新月，在某个不平静的夜晚，
受海潮的召唤，又会露出脸儿。

Each that we lose takes part of us;
A crescent still abides,
Which like the moon, some turbid night,
Is summoned by the tides.

迷津（NO.224）

你知道——我没有别的东西——送你，
所以我总是带来这些——
就像夜晚给我们司空见惯了的眼睛
一再地把星星带来——

也许，我们不会将它们留意——
只要它们还出现在天空——
否则——在回家的路上，我们或许
就要走入了迷津——

I've nothing else — to bring, You know —
So I keep bringing These —
Just as the Night keeps fetching Stars
To our familiar eyes —

Maybe, we shouldn't mind them —
Unless they didn't come —
Then — maybe, it would puzzle us
To find our way Home —

心儿有窄窄的堤岸（NO.928）

心儿有窄窄的堤岸
它[①]似海一般的宽阔
有力——不停地低声鸣唱
一片单调的蓝色

直到飓风来至将它劈开
在它自己发现出
它空间的不足时
痉挛的心儿开始悟出

平静只是一层未经
触动的薄薄的锦帛
偶尔的一推一搡或是
一个疑团——都能将其捅破。

---

① 指海。

The Heart has narrow Banks
It measures like the Sea
In mighty — unremitting Bass
And Blue Monotony

Till Hurricane bisect
And as itself discerns
Its sufficient Area
The Heart convulsive learns

That Calm is but a Wall
Of unattempted Gauze
An instant's Push demolishes
A Questioning — dissolves.

暴风雨的夜（NO.249）

暴风雨的夜啊——暴风雨的夜！
如果我现在与你[①]相伴
暴风雨的夜晚就会是
我们共同的消遣！

劲风——变得无用——
对一个栖在岸上的心灵——
它已离开了航海图——
离开了指南针！

啊，大海！
如果我今晚能停留
在你的怀中
我会像是在伊甸园里划舟！

① 指大海。

Wild Nights — Wild Nights!
Were I with thee
Wild Nights should be
Our luxury!

Futile — the Winds —
To a Heart in port —
Done with the Compass —
Done with the Chart!

Rowing in Eden —
Ah, the Sea!
Might I but moor — Tonight —
In Thee!

虚幻（NO.739）

有许多次我以为平和已经来临
当平和还离我很远时——
就如在深海里遇险的人——
以为他们看到了陆地——

于是开始松了口气——结果只是
像我一样无望地发现——
在抵达港湾之前
还有多少似岸的虚景在诱哄你——

I many times thought Peace had come
When Peace was far away —
As Wrecked Men — deem they sight the Land —
At Centre of the Sea —

And struggle slacker — but to prove
As hopelessly as I —
How many the fictitious Shores —
Before the Harbor be —

狂喜（NO.76）

狂喜是一个内陆的心灵
在去到大海，
经过了房舍——经过了田野的畦垄——
进到永恒的存在

海上的水手能理解
山里长大的我们
在刚刚离开陆地
驶入大海时的激奋心情吗？

Exultation is the going
Of an inland soul to sea,
Past the houses — past the headlands —
Into deep Eternity —

Bred as we, among the mountains,
Can the sailor understand
The divine intoxication
Of the first league out from land?

大海对小溪说（NO.1210）

大海对小溪说“快来吧”——
小溪说“先让我长大”——
大海说“那样你也将变成海——
我要的是溪流——来吧”！

大海说“快归入”大海——
大海说“我正是你所向往的”
“渊博的海洋——智慧
对我显得迂腐”[①]，小溪说。

① 作者想让我们的头脑像小溪那样，永远保持着新鲜活泼；不因为具有渊博的学问就变得有了书卷气。

The Sea said "Come" to the Brook —
The Brook said "Let me grow" —
The Sea said "Then you will be a Sea —
I want a Brook — Come now"!

The Sea said "Go" to the Sea —
The Sea said "I am he
You cherished" — "Learned Waters —
Wisdom is stale — to Me"

飘荡（NO.30）

飘荡！一只小船在飘荡！
夜晚正在来临！
有谁会把小船
引航到就近的小镇？

海员们说——昨天——
在阴沉沉的暮霭中
一只小船放弃了拼搏
随海浪飘泊浮沉。

天使们说——昨天——
于红色的朝霞里
一只小船——饱经了暴风雨的磨难——
修好了桅杆——重扯起风帆——
又在精神抖擞加速向前！

Adrift! A little boat adrift!
And night is coming down!
Will no one guide a little boat
Unto the nearest town?

So Sailors say — on yesterday —
Just as the dusk was brown
One little boat gave up its strife
And gurgled down and down.

So angels say — on yesterday —
Just as the dawn was red
One little boat — o'erspent with gales —
Retrimmed its masts — redecked its sails —
And shot — exultant on!

很小的船（NO.107）

这是一只很小——很小的船
在颠簸着驶出海港！
这是一个多浩瀚——多浩瀚的海
在招手邀它驶向远方！

这是多么贪婪，贪婪的海浪
在舔触着船儿离开海滨——
也不管有多少次远航
我的小船迷失在海中！

'Twas such a little — little boat
That toddled down the bay!
'Twas such a gallant — gallant sea
That beckoned it away!

'Twas such a greedy, greedy wave
That licked it from the Coast —
Nor ever guessed the stately sails
My little craft was lost!

蹒跚（NO.875）

我从一块木板迈到另一块木板
慢慢地小心地举步
我觉得星星在我的周围闪烁
大海在我的脚下起伏。

我只知道我的下一脚也许
就是我的最后一步——
这给予我那种蹒跚的步态
有人称其为经验。

I stepped from Plank to Plank
A slow and cautious way
The Stars about my Head I felt
About my Feet the Sea.

I knew not but the next
Would be my final inch —
This gave me that precarious Gait
Some call Experience.

经验（NO.910）

经验是一条定向之路
它宁愿反对人的头脑
然而——正是头脑自己
以为它将经验指导

情形恰恰相反——世事多难料
人生多磨炼——
这些都迫使他要为自己选择
他已注定的苦难——

Experience is the Angled Road
Preferred against the Mind
By — Paradox — the Mind itself —
Presuming it to lead

Quite Opposite — How Complicate
The Discipline of Man —
Compelling Him to Choose Himself
His Preappointed Pain —

就像你知道那是正午（NO.420）

你会识别出它的——就像你知道那是正午——
凭着其灿烂的光华——
就像你知道这是太阳——
凭借其四射的光芒——
就像你到了天堂——
会认出上帝和他的儿子基督一样。

强大的事物藉其本能
而不是言辞得到显扬——
用着夜晚说——“我是子夜”——
用着太阳说——“我是日出”吗？

造化——不用语言——
闪电雷霆是他的——发音——
大海的涛声——是他的讲话——
“你怎么知道的呢？”
请用你的眼睛！

You'll know it — as you know 'tis Noon —
By Glory —
As you do the Sun —
By Glory —
As you will in Heaven —
Know God the Father — and the Son.

By intuition, Mightiest Things
Assert themselves — and not by terms —
"I'm Midnight" — need the Midnight say —
"I'm Sunrise" — Need the Majesty?

Omnipotence — had not a Tongue —
His listp — is Lightning — and the Sun —
His Conversation — with the Sea —
"How shall you know"?
Consult your Eye!

沿着时间这条特别的河（NO.1656）

沿着时间这条特别的河
我们没有桨橹
不得不顺势航行
我们要去的港湾还是个谜
我们的前面就可能是飓风
是什么样的船长为我们导航
会不会把我们引入险境
什么样的海盗也在飘行
而且风向变换
潮汐无定——

Down Time's quaint stream
Without an oar
We are enforced to sail
Our Port a secret
Our Perchance a Gale
What Skipper would
Incur the Risk
What Buccaneer would ride
Without a surety from the Wind
Or schedule of the Tide —

英雄主义（NO.1176）

我们从不知道自己有多么高大
直到我们应情势的需要而升起
那时如果我们又执着于理想
我们的身躯就能倚天而立——

我们咏诵不已的英雄主义
将会变为平常之事
只要不是因为我们怕当国王
硬是用腕尺羁缚了自己——

We never know how high we are
Till we are asked to rise
And then if we are true to plan
Our statures touch the skies —

The Heroism we recite
Would be a normal thing
Did not ourselves the Cubits warp
For fear to be a King —

成功的甜蜜（NO.67）

成功的甜蜜最受
未成功者的品尝，
要能品咂出美酒的香醇
需有强烈的嗜酒的欲望。

今天军队里的
穿紫色军服的扛旗人
没有一个能更确切地
把胜利的含义界定

比之于受挫快要死去的士兵
在他那急切聆听的耳畔
远处的胜利进行曲
正痛苦而又清晰地回旋！

Success is counted sweetest
By those who ne'er succeed.
To comprehend a nectar
Requires sorest need.

Not one of all the purple Host
Who took the Flag today
Can tell the definition
So clear of Victory

As he defeated — dying —
On whose forbidden ear
The distant strains of triumph
Burst agonized and clear!

人的成长（NO.750）

人的成长——就像自然的生长——
是受内里的驱动——
虽然大气和阳光给以佐助——
可它[①]独自——动于中——

难以达到的理想——必须
通过自己——去实现——
通过默默无闻的甘受
寂寞的顽强和自勉——

拼搏——是首要的条件——
还有自我克制——
对诸种冲突力量的静观——
以及不渝的信念——

旁观——是其观众的
职责范围——
要达到成功——不能凭借任何
外面的鼓励——

① 指生长。

Growth of Man — like Growth of Nature —

Gravitates within —

Atmosphere, and Sun endorse it —

Bit it stir — alone —

Each — its difficult Ideal

Must achieve — Itself —

Through the solitary prowess

Of a Silent Life —

Effort — is the sole condition —

Patience of Itself —

Patience of opposing forces —

And intact Belief —

Looking on — is the Department

Of its Audience —

But Transaction — is assisted

By no Countenance —

成功已来得太迟·无韵诗（NO.690）

成功已来得太迟——
它俯身到已冰冷的嘴唇——
唇儿因结满霜冻
已对它无法品尝——
要是能尝一尝它那甜甜的滋味——
那怕只是一滴——
难道上帝就如此吝啬？
他把餐桌上的食物摆得太高——
我们只有踮起脚去够——

碎屑——适合于小小的喙——
樱桃——适合于知更鸟儿——
苍鹰丰盛的早餐只会把它们——噎着——
上帝对麻雀守着他的诺言——
因不懂爱抚的麻雀——知道如何挨过饥饿——

Victory comes late —
And is held low to freezing lips —
Too rapt with frost
To take it —
How sweet it would have tasted —
Just a Drop —
Was God so economical?
His Table's spread too high for Us —
Unless We dine on tiptoe —

Crumbs — fit such little mouths —
Cherries — suit Robbins —
The Eagle's Golden Breakfast strangles — Them —
God keep His Oath to Sparrows —
Who of little Love — know how to starve —

白昼有什么用（NO.611）

在黑暗里——我看你更清楚——
我不需要灯盏——
我对你的爱——便是一个棱晶体——
远胜过紫罗兰——

日子越久我看你越清楚
岁月间相隆起留下印迹——
矿工的灯儿——便足能——
驱除井下的漆黑——

在坟茔里——我看你最清楚——
狭小的墓壁处处
生辉——红彤彤——因我为你
把灯火高举——

白昼有什么用——
对那些处在黑暗而感觉胜似有阳光的人——
这样，他们的正午[①]——不就是——
永无止境？

① 喻全盛期。

I see thee better — in the Dark —
I do not need a Light —
The Love of Thee — a Prism be —
Excelling Violet —

I see thee better for the Years
That hunch themselves between —
The Miner's Lamp — sufficient be —
To nullify the Mine —

And in the Grave — I see Thee best —
Its little Panels be
Aglow — All ruddy — with the Light
I held so high, for Thee —

What need of Day —
To Those whose Dark — hath so — surpassing Sun —
It deem it be — Continually —
At the Meridian?

凡我能做的（NO.361）

凡我能做的——我将为之——
纵使事情小得像一朵水仙花儿——
凡我不能做的——一定是
其实现的可能性尚不被人知晓——

What I can do — I will —
Though it be little as a Daffodil —
That I cannot — must be
Unknown to possibility —

不要作茧自缚（NO.720）

不要作茧自缚——
当自由他自己——
和你——在一起的时候——

No Prisoner be —
Where Liberty —
Himself — abide with Thee —

永恒（NO.680）

每个生命都在朝着某个中心汇集——
无论是已显露——还是蛰伏着——
总有一个目标在每个人身上
存活——

或许——它[①]对它自己也不十分清楚——
它太美太美
不愿意让“相信”恣意
将它损毁——

我们小心地膜拜它——像对易碎的天堂——
要想达到没有希望，
就像我们无法摸着
彩虹的衣裳——

---

① 代指目标。

然而——坚定地——我们追求不已——
苍天——
对于我们这些朝圣者的笨拙的努力
显得高不可攀——

人生于尘世的冒险——也许——达不到目标——
不过到那时——
永恒又会叫这一努力
重新做起。

Each Life Converges to some Centre —
Expressed — or still —
Exists in every Human Nature
A Goal —

Embodied scarcely to itself — it may be —
Too fair
For Credibility's presumption
To mar —

Adored with caution — as a Brittle Heaven —
To reach
Were hopeless, as the Rainbow's Raiment
To touch —

Yet persevered toward — sure — for the Distance —

How high —

Unto the Saint's slow diligence —

The Sky —

Ungained — it may be — by a Life's low Venture —

But then —

Eternity enable the endeavoring

Again.

飞鸟（NO.703）

已经不在视线之内？那又怎么样？
瞧，小鸟——正在把它追上！
她时而盘绕回旋——时而上下俯冲
于大气之间——
危险！那又奈她如何？
失败在——蓝天——
总比在这里无谓的争辩——好些——

蔚蓝烘托着蔚蓝—— 一望无际——
下面是琥珀色——琥珀色的——露水——
朋友——你若探寻——就会发觉——
苍穹对大地害羞——
啊羞怯的苍穹——你的渺小的
崇拜者们——也在——把你躲避——

Out of sight? What of that?
See the Bird — reach it!
Curve by Curve — Sweep by Sweep —
Round the Steep Air —
Danger! What is that to Her?
Better 'tis to fail — there —
Than debate — here —

Blue is Blue — the World through —
Amber — Amber — Dew — Dew —
Seek — Friend — and see —
Heaven is shy of Earth — that's all —
Bashful Heaven — thy Lovers small —
Hide — too — from thee —

逃（NO.77）

每当听到“逃走”这个词儿时
我血液的流动就会加快，
突然而至的期盼，
一个飞的姿态！

每当听到偌大的监狱
被士兵们捣毁，
我总会稚气地摇动铁窗，不过，
只是再一次体味了失败而已！

I never hear the word "escape"
Without a quicker blood,
A sudden expectation
A flying attitude!

I never hear of prisons broad
By soldiers battered down,
But I tug childish at my bars
Only to fail again!

失败与冒险（NO.847）

失败——是有限的，可冒险是无限的——
为一只船舰威风凛凛地返航靠岸
多少英勇无畏的斗士——被海水吞没
永不能再在队列中出现——

Finite — to fail, but infinite to Venture —
For the one ship that struts the shore
Many's the gallant — overwhelmed Creature
Nodding in Navies nevermore —

心扉（NO.1214）

我们向花朵和行星
敞开心扉
可是当我们面对自己时
我们却行起繁缛的礼节
变得尴尬与
唯喏起来

We introduce ourselves
To Planets and to Flowers
But with ourselves
Have etiquettes
Embarrassments
And awes

真的穷困（NO.771）

没有谁能真正体验到了节制
如果他还不知道——富足
饥荒的事实——如果没有五谷丰登的
事实佐证也不能算数——

匮乏——是贫瘠的艺术
它从其相反的那面得到——
没有尝过富裕的穷困——
不是真正的穷愁潦倒。

None can experience sting
Who Bounty — have not known —
The fact of Famine — could not be
Except for Fact of Corn —

Want — is a meagre Art
Acquired by Reverse —
The Poverty that was not Wealth —
Cannot be Indigence.

拼搏（NO.126）

呐喊着去拼杀，固然很勇敢——
不过，我知道，更为英勇的
是那些跟内心的万般痛苦
进行的拼搏——

这种拼搏，胜了，国人看不到——
失败了——也无人知晓——
于他弥留之际，没有人会把他
当作爱国的英杰来瞧——

我们相信，在排列成阵的队伍里
天使们，正是为此——
前赴后继，行着稳健的脚步——
身着雪白的羽衣。

To fight aloud, is very brave —
But gallanter, I know
Who charge within the bosom
The Cavalry of Woe —

Who win, and nations do not see —
Who fall — and none observe —
Whose dying eyes, no Country
Regards with patriot love —

We trust, in plumed procession
For such, the Angels go —
Rank after Rank, with even feet —
And Uniforms of Snow.

我要整个苍穹（NO.352）

也许我的要求太大——
我要——整个苍穹——
因为地上已变得繁密，
恰如我家乡的草莓——

我的篮子里——装得下——这些天空——
它们——在我的胳膊上——轻快地摇晃，
可是一些小小的杂物便能把它塞得很满。

Perhaps I asked too large —

I take — no less than skies —

For Earths, grow thick as

Berries, in my native town —

My Basked holds — just — Firmaments —

Those — dangle easy — on my arm,

But smaller bundles — Cram.

在灯拿掉以后（NO.419）

在灯拿掉以后我们慢慢
会习惯了黑暗——
恰如邻居举着灯火
送我们出了庭院——

有一会儿——我们在这新夜里
会小心地走路——
随后——视力适应了黑暗——
我们便迈开——大步——

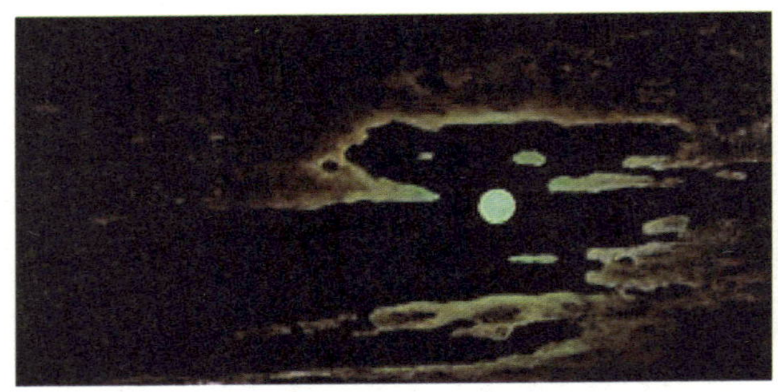

在我们的头脑里有时也会有——
这样的黑暗——这样的夜晚——
那里没有星星闪烁——
也没有月亮——露脸——

勇敢的——会摸索着前进——
有时会迎头
撞上一棵大树——
但是一段的探索之后——

不是黑暗有了改变——
就是我们矫正了视力
慢慢地适应了长夜——
这时生命的步子便会迈直。

We grow accustomed to the Dark —
When light is put away —
As when the Neighbor holds the Lamp
To witness her Goodbye —

A Moment — We uncertain step
For newness of the night —
Then — fit our Vision to the Dark —
And meet the Road — erect —

And so of larger — Darkness —
Those Evenings of the Brain —
When not a Moon disclose a sign —
Or Star — come out — within —

The Bravest — grope a little —
And sometimes hit a Tree
Directly in the Forehead —
But as they learn to see —

Either the Darkness alters —
Or something in the sight
Adjusts itself to Midnight —
And Life steps almost straight.

逝去（NO.1083）

我们于心情失落时晓得了
一个多么伟大的人
不久前曾在我们中间
一颗陨落的恒星

在逝去时我们才觉其珍贵
多少倍
珍贵于它生前的
所有——光辉——

We learn it in Retreating
How vast an one
Was recently among us —
A Perished Sun

Endear in the departure
How doubly more
Than all the Golden presence
It was — before—

内在（NO.451）

外象——从内里
得到它的恢宏——
是公爵，是侏儒，取决于
其主要的禀性——

是精制的——不渝的轴
控制着轮子的运行——
尽管辐条——更耀人眼目的——旋转
而且不时地扬起——飞尘。

是内在——画出外表——
恰如神的画笔自主——
精确地——绘出了
其所思所悟——

于天造地设的——画布上——
我们的眼睛不是用来知晓——
一副面庞——一个额头——
或是映在湖里的——星星的奥妙。

The Outer — from the Inner
Derives its Magnitude —
'Tis Duke, or Dwarf, according
As is the Central Mood —

The fine — unvarying Axis
That regulates the Wheel —
Though Spokes — spin — more conspicuous
And fling a dust — the while.

The Inner — paints the Outer —
The Brush without the Hand —
Its Picture publishes — precise —
As is the inner Brand —

On fine — Arterial Canvas —
A Cheek — perchance a Brow —
The Star's whole Secret — in the Lake —
Eyes were not meant to know.

秘密（NO.191）

天空保守不住它们的秘密！
它们把它告诉了山峦——
山峦告诉了果园——
果园——告诉了水仙！

一只鸟儿——正巧——经过那里——
听到了这个秘密的全部——
如果我贿赂一下小鸟——
谁知道她会不会把秘密告诉我？

不过——我觉得我不会那么做——
还是不知道的——更好——
如果夏天是——自明之理——
下雪又岂会有什么妖道？

所以守住你的秘密吧——上帝！
即便我能——我也不会去探知
在你那新造的世界里
玉男玉女们的所做所为！

The Skies can't keep their secret!
They tell it to the Hills —
The Hills just tell the Orchards —
And they — the Daffodils!

A Bird — by chance — that goes that way —
Soft overhears the whole —
If I should bribe the little Bird —
Who knows but she would tell?

I think I won't — however —
It's finer — not to know —
If Summer were an Axiom —
What sorcery had Snow?

So keep your secret — Father!
I would not — if I could,
Know what the Sapphire Fellows, do,
In your new-fashioned world!

最美的诗意（NO.1472）

眺望夏日的天空就是最美的诗章，
尽管它没有出现在任何的书本里——
真正的诗歌会飞——

To see the Summer Sky
Is Poetry, though never in a Book it lie —
True Poems flee —

真理（NO.1472）

说出所有的真理但不要径直倒出——
成功接通着巨大的电流
其辉煌一下子让我们无以受用
真理给人的惊奇巨大无偶

就像闪电对于孩子，唯有经过解释
才能减轻了他们的惊恐
真理的光芒须渐渐地闪耀起来
否则会弄瞎了每个人的眼睛——

Tell all the Truth but tell it slant —
Success in Circuit lies
Too bright for our infirm Delight
The Truth's superb surprise

As Lightning to the Children eased
With explanation kind
The Truth must dazzle gradually
Or every man be blind —

孤独与喧嚣

Lonely and Noisy

无名之人（NO.288）

我是个无名的人！你呢？
你——也是——无名的人吗？
那么便有一对这样的人啦！
且不要说出！你知道他们会张扬，为我们俩！

做个——名人——多乏味！
整天价——招摇——
像只六月的青蛙——对着仰慕它的池塘——
不休地炫耀！

I'm Nobody! Who are you?
Are you — Nobody — Too?
Then there's a pair of us!
Don't tell! they'd advertise — you know!

How dreary — to be — Somebody!
How public — like a Frog —
To tell one's name — the livelong June —
To an admiring Bog!

孤寂（NO.405）

那会更加的孤寂
如果孤独离开了我——
我习惯了我现在的命运
或许另外的一种——祥和——

会侵扰了这里的黑暗——
他[①]进来，那小小的空间——
会太拥挤——无法再容下
供奉他的——祭坛——

我已经不再习惯于“希望”——
它会是不速之客——
它的光顾——只会冒犯了
命定罹难的这儿——

有陆地在望
而失败于——海上——
要好于我到达了——蓝色的岛屿——
因高兴——而衰亡——

① 指祥和。

It might be lonelier
Without the Loneliness —
I'm so accustomed to my Fate —
Perhaps the Other — Peace —

Would interrupt the Dark —
And crowd the little Room —
Too scant — by Cubits — to contain
The Sacrament — of Him —

I am not used to Hope —
It might intrude upon —
Its sweet parade — blaspheme the place —
Ordained to Suffering —

It might be easier
To fail — with Land in Sight —
Than gain — My Blue Peninsula —
To perish — of Delight —

孤独的深浅（NO.777）

人不敢测量孤独的深浅——
顶多粗粗地臆断一下
就像到它的墓穴里要胆战心惊地
量出它的尺码——

孤独最害怕的就是
看到它自己——
就是衰竭于对它自己
所做的谛视——

这一恐怖没有谁敢直面——
只能是把意识悬搁——
并加上锁，然后摸黑——
悄悄地绕过——

我猜想这——便是孤独——
无论是造物主
照亮着还是封闭着
它[1]的通廊和洞岫——

① 指孤独。

The Loneliness One dare not sound —
And would as soon surmise
As in its Grave go plumbing
To ascertain the size —

The Loneliness whose worst alarm
Is lest itself should see —
And perish from before itself
For just a scrutiny —

The Horror not to be surveyed —
But skirted in the Dark —
With Consciousness suspended —
And Being under Lock —

I fear me this — is Loneliness —
The Maker of the soul
Its Caverns and its Corridors
Illuminate — or seal —

另一种孤独（NO.1116）

这儿还有另外的一种孤独
许多人至死也没有体尝到——
这孤独不是由于缺少朋友
或环境运气的坏与好

而是源于自然，有时是灵感
有自然之灵感降至的人
它的富足无法用通常的
数字单位计衡——

There is another Loneliness
That many die without —
Not want of friend occasions it
Or circumstances of Lot

But nature, sometimes, sometimes thought
And whoso it befall
Is richer than could be revealed
By mortal numeral —

家门（NO.609）

我已离开家多年
现在到了家门前
我不敢走入，免得一张
我从未见过的脸

冷峻地把我直视
问我为何闯进了这里——
“我以前曾在这儿生活过
我来是想看看旧日的温馨是否还在？”

我心中满是畏惧——
过去在我脑中流连——
秒针的滴答声如大洋的翻卷
敲打着我的耳鼓——

我发出一阵撕裂的笑声
我竟然会害怕一扇门
我这个经历过千惊万险
而从未退缩过的人。

我把颤栗的手
小心翼翼地伸进门栓
担心这倒楣的门反弹回来
会把我撞倒在地——

然后移动我的手，轻轻地
仿佛在搬动一块玻璃，
我竖耳倾听，临了像个小偷一样
喘嘘嘘地逃离了那所房子——

I Years had been from Home
And now before the Door
I dared not enter, lest a Face
I never saw before

Stare solid into mine
And ask my Business there —
"My Business but a Life I left
Was such remaining there?"

I leaned upon the Awe —
I lingered with Before —
The Second like an Ocean rolled
And broke against my ear —

I laughed a crumbling Laugh
That I could fear a Door
Who Consternation compassed
And never winced before.

I fitted to the Latch
My Hand, with trembling care
Lest back the awful Door should spring
And leave me in the Floor —

Then moved my Fingers off
As cautiously as Glass
And held my ears, and like a Thief
Fled gasping from the House —

晚归（NO.207）

尽管我很晚——很晚才能回家去——
我还是要回去——因为我将得到补偿——
这样的憧憬令人激奋：
他们等我已等得心冷——
夜晚——降临——漆黑——而又宁静——
蓦然，他们意料之外地听到了敲门声——
由漫长的痛苦酝酿而致——
这一刻一定令人迷醉！

想想柴火会怎样的燃烧作响——
已等待无望的眼睛会转过来如何看我——
猜想我会如何地辩说，
家人又会对我如何地数落——
这真能消磨掉我无数的时刻！

Tho' I get home how late — how late —

So I get home — 'twill compensate —

Better will be the Ecstasy

That they have done expecting me —

When Night — descending — dumb — and dark —

They hear my unexpected knock —

Transporting must the moment be —

Brewed from decades of Agony!

To think just how the fire will burn —

Just how long-cheated eyes will turn —

To wonder what myself will say,

And what itself, will say to me —

Beguiles the Centuries of way!

羁缚（NO.613）

他们把我羁缚在乏味的平淡之中
就像当年我还是个小女孩时
他们关我在壁橱里——
唯有我“安静”他们才欢喜——

“安静”！如若他们往里面窥视——
看见我头脑的——不停的活动
他们便会晓得他们是在把一只鸟儿
囚在了——围栏中——

只要它自己愿意
它就可以像星星那样
轻易地摆脱对它的束缚——
啼唱着——去自由地翱翔——

They shut me up in Prose —
As when a little Girl
They put me in the Closet —
Because they liked me "still" —

Still! Could themself have peeped —
And seen my Brain — go round —
They might as wise have lodged a Bird
For Treason — in the Pound —

Himself has but to will
And easy as a Star
Abolish his Captivity —
And laugh — No more have I —

长长的一觉（NO.654）

长长的一觉——不俗的一觉——
对早晨没有任何的表示——
四肢不伸——眼睑无动——
一任其自己——
可有过这样的逍遥？
在石头的堤岸上
晒太阳晒得不知今夕是何年——
从不曾抬眼看过——正午的太阳？

A long — long Sleep — A famous — Sleep —
That makes no show for Morn —
By Stretch of Limb — or stir of Lid —
An independent One —
Was ever idleness like This?
Upon a Bank of Stone
To bask the Centuries away —
Nor once look up — for Noon?

耐心（NO.926）

耐心——有个平静的外表——
耐心——如果窥视到它的里面——
则似昆虫于无垠的——冥冥之间——
所施的种种徒劳的努力——

幸免于这一个——却更狠地
把另一个撞着——
耐心——是在颤栗中间
掬出的微笑——

Patience — has a quiet Outer —
Patience — Look within —
Is an Insect's futile forces
Infinites — between —

'Scaping one — against the other
Fruitlesser to fling —
Patience — is the Smile's exertion
Through the quivering —

清扫（NO.1273）

当你清扫那个称之为“记忆”的
神圣柜橱时——
要选一把虔诚的笤帚——
肃穆地为之。

这将是一种充满惊奇的劳作——
除了会鉴别出
许多其他的人和事
还会有可能性把头探出——

这一领地的灰尘很是威严
最好还是不要动它——让它躺着——
你不能将它取而代之
它却能叫你沉默——

That sacred Closet when you sweep —
Entitled "Memory" —
Select a reverential Broom —
And do it silently.

'T will be a Labor of surprise —
Besides Identity
Of other Interlocutors
A probability —

August the Dust of that Domain —
Unchallenged — let it lie —
You cannot supersede itself
But it can silence you —

我们穿小了爱（NO.887）

我们穿小了“爱”，于是像其他物件一样
我们把它放进柜里——
直待到时尚返古又时新起它[①]
恰如祖辈的服饰有时又会流行起来。

We outgrow love, like other things
And put it in the Drawer —
Till it an Antique fashion shows —
Like Costumes Grandsires wore.

① 指爱。此诗也可说是对那种把“爱”当作时尚而不是发自心底的人的一种讽刺。

风险（NO.1678）

把风险作为一种拥有[①]
去对待，较为明智
危险会肢解了你的餍足感
居安思危会使你
产生一种畏惧
把人性中的积垢痼习
剔除得一点不留。

Peril as a Possesssion
'Tis Good to hear
Danger disintegrates Satiety
There's Basis there —
Begets an awe
That searches Human Nature's creases
As clean as Fire.

① 原文是 Possession，这里有财富之意。

我敬畏（NO.543）

我敬畏不苟言谈的人
我敬畏缄默的人——
嘴碎者——我能坦然处之——
对高谈阔论者——我能制胜——

而当众人——都在一掷千金的时候——
唯他却能权衡再三——
对此人我就会小心——
我敬畏他的伟岸——

I fear a Man of frugal Speech —
I fear a Silent Man —
Haranguer — I can overtake —
Or Babbler — entertain —

But He who weigheth — While the Rest —
Expend their furthest pound —
Of this Man — I am wary —
I fear that He is Grand —

意会（NO.1048）

那些只能意会的主题，不停地向
聪慧者的心田里输入——
可对于其余的人，却难以理解得
像是丹麦人的土语。

那些奥妙的音律，对于敏感的
耳朵——是美好的刺激——
对于其他的人却犹如是
东方的寓言，古怪离奇——

Reportless Subjects, to the Quick
Continual addressed —
But foreign as the Dialect
Of Danes, unto the rest.

Reportless Measures, to the Ear
Susceptive — stimulus —
But like an Oriental Tale
To others, fabulous —

贵贱（NO.1240）

上门来讨名声的乞丐
很容易就能求得
可面包却要比前者圣洁得多
乞讨者很可能被拒绝

The Beggar at the Door for Fame
Were easily supplied
But Bread is that Diviner thing
Disclosed to be denied

生命与生命的差别（NO.1101）

生命与生命之间存在着很大的差别
犹如溢在瓶嘴的酒
和盛在罐中的酒的区别
后者——最适合于保存——
可是为了享用消受
无塞的酒则更胜一筹——
我尝试过所以我知道

Between the form of Life and Life
The difference is as big
As Liquor at the Lip between
And Liquor in the Jug
The latter — excellent to keep —
But for ecstatic need
The corkless is superior —
I know for I have tried

把戏（NO.688）

“言辞”——是一种议会里玩的把戏
“眼泪”——是神经使用的计谋——
不过负荷太重的心灵——
并不总是——那么——易受感触——

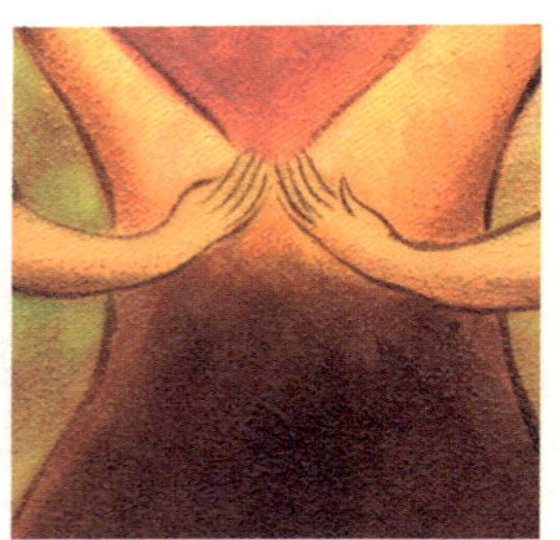

“Speech” — is a prank of Parliament —
“Tears” — is a trick of the nerve —
But the Heart with the heaviest freight on —
Doesn’t — always — move —

平常事（NO.741）

在我们周围发生着的平常之事
是戏剧的最富生命力的表达——
其他的悲剧

消失在了表演中间——
这一种——却进行得最在兴头
当剧院拉下帷幕
观众散去以后——

对其[①]而言，“哈姆雷特”仍还是哈姆雷特——
即使莎士比亚没有将它写出——
这样，尽管“罗米欧”就不会有
朱丽叶的故事传后，

可是这类事仍会在人类的心灵里
永远地进行——
剧本只是做了记载
主人也不能关上看门——

① 指哈姆雷特。

Drama's Vitallest Expression is the Common Day

That arise and set about Us —

Other Tragedy

Perish in the Recitation —

This — the best enact

When the Audience is scattered

And the Boxes shut —

"Hamlet" to Himself were Hamlet —

Had not Shakespeare wrote —

Though the "Romeo" left no Record

Of his Juliet,

It were infinite enacted

In the Human Heart —

Only Theatre recorded

Owner cannot shut —

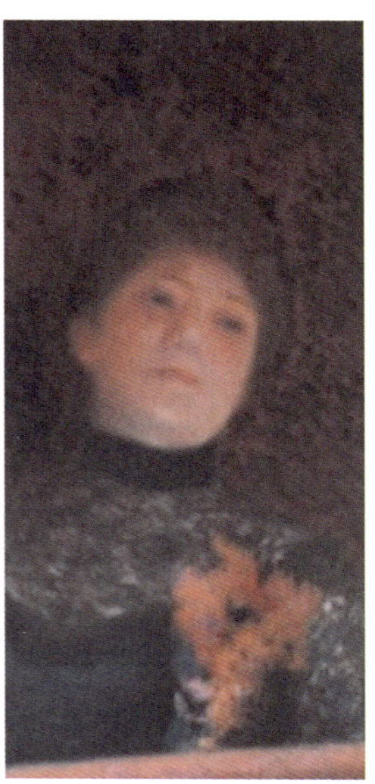

丰盛与赤贫（NO.1189）

在我听似春潮迸涌的声音
一些人却充耳不闻——
叫灿烂的早晨失色的面庞其妩媚
却不能使他们有动于衷——

这里实质性的不同在于
对我是丰盛的东西
在那些金融家看来
却是赤贫如洗！

The Voice that stands for Floods to me

Is sterile borne to some —

The Face that makes the Morning mean

Glows impotent on them —

What difference in Substance lies

That what is Sum to me

By other Financiers be deemed

Exclusive Property!

荒凉（NO.1147）

经过了百十年后
没有人再认识这个地方
曾于这里肆虐的悲苦
已平了声息归于安详

这儿曾经野草萋萋
陌路人也曾徜徉于此
对着前人的荒凉坟茔
试着仔细地品味

唯有夏日田野上的风
能将那段历史记起——
本能捡起了记忆
掉落的钥匙——

After a hundred years
Nobody knows the Place
Agony that enacted there
Motionless as Peace

Weeds triumphant ranged
Strangers strolled and spelled
At the lone Orthography
Of the Elder Dead

Winds of Summer Fields
Recollect the way —
Instinct picking up the Key
Dropped by memory —

未开始（NO.1088）

还没开始，已经终结——
题目刚被说出
序章就从意识中消失
故事，没有泄漏——

如果它能成为我的，被出版问世！
如果它能成为你的，供你阅读！
可上帝早已给了训谕说
他未把这一特权赐予你我——

Ended, ere it begun —

The Title was scarcely told

When the Preface perished from Consciousness

The Story, unrevealed —

Had it been mine, to print!

Had it been yours, to read!

That it was not Our privilege

The interdict of God —

聊胜于无（NO.1089）

我自己能读这些电文
它们是我的主要信件
证券股票的涨跌
市场行情的走势

还有天气——乡下的雨季
今年又如何开始。
这些消息全无用处，
不过仍觉甜蜜——什么也无法相比。

Myself can read the Telegrams
A Letter chief to me
The Stock's advance and Retrograde
And what the Markets say

The Weather — how the Rains
In Counties have begun.
'Tis News as null as nothing,
But sweeter so — than none.

犹豫（NO.830）

她又回到了这个世界。
不过却多了一个特征——
一种多重的仪态举止，
就像土壤
娶了紫罗兰
紫罗兰却主要是向着天空
而不是跟他自己，联姻，
她居在中间犹豫不决，这位一半
属于土壤一半属于阳光的新娘。

To this World she returned.

But with a tinge of that —

A Compound manner,

As a Sod

Espoused a Violet,

That chiefer to the Skies

Than to himself, allied,

Dwelt hesitating, half of Dust,

And half of Day, the Bride.

名声是一种无常的食物（NO.1659）

名声是一种无常的食物
盛在一个移动的盘子里
一位客人偶尔支起了
放它的桌子
就再也没有出现过

乌鸦看到了桌上的碎屑
讥嘲地聒叫着
用翅膀将它扇到了
农家的谷物里——
吃了它的人们都死掉了。

Fame is a fickle food
Upon a shifting plate
Whose table once a
Guest but not
The second time is set.

Whose crumbs the crows inspect
And with ironic caw
Flap past it to the
Farmer's Corn —
Men eat of it and die.

得到名声的方式（NO.1427）

用不屑于理会它的方式来得到它
是付给名声的最好的入场券——
他[①]喜爱对他排斥的东西——
不信，往后看——他正在把你追赶。

所以让我们一起——日积月累地——
采撷生活的花蕾
诚实地做人，
不至将来后悔——

① 指名声。

To earn it by disdaining it
Is Fame's consummate Fee —
He loves what spurns him —
Look behind — He is pursuing thee.

So let us gather — every Day —
The Aggregate of
Life's Bouquet
Be Honor and not shame —

沟渠（NO.1645）

沟渠对醉酒的人尤其亲近
因为它不就是他的床——
他的拥戴者——他的大厦吗？
他倒地的头多么的安然无恙
在这一脏乱不堪的圣地——
他的上面是蓝天
“忘却”俯身抚慰着他
名誉利禄都离开他好远。

The Ditch is dear to the Drunken man

For is it not his Bed —

His Advocate — his Edifice?

How safe his fallen Head

In her disheveled Sanctity —

Above him is the sky —

Oblivion bending over him

And Honor leagues away.

不妄为的生活（NO.696）

他们的高高在上并不能叫我艳羡——
他们的荣耀——我不屑一顾——
澹泊淡雅——这样就好——
我不盼顾——不觊觎

异想天开的巨厦——
围绕着可能性的疆域
发出熠熠光亮的边缘——
在我看——显得很不牢固——

我现有的财富——已使我满足——
如果它只是很寒酸的一点儿——
那我也会爱不释手，如数家珍——
直到它把我的眼睛愉悦——

这远胜于价值连城——
不管它[①]显得好像有多么真实——
这一脚踏实地的不妄为的生活
总在说——“我对它一点儿也不知。”

① 指价值连城。

Their Height in Heaven comforts not —
Their Glory — nought to me —
'Twas best imperfect — as it was —
I'm finite — I can't see —

The House of Supposition —
The Glimmering Frontier that
Skirts the Acres of Perhaps —
To Me — shows insecure —

The Wealth I had — contented me —
If 'twas a meaner size —
Then I had counted it until
It pleased my narrow Eyes —

Better than larger values —
That show however true —
This timid life of Evidence
Keeps pleading — "I don't know."

宴请（NO.579）

这些年来，我总在挨饿——
终于，我等来了宴请的——日子——
我颤巍巍地挨近到饭桌——
触到了琼浆玉液——

这些美食我曾经见过——
在我空腹走回家的路上
我眼巴巴地瞧望橱窗里面
那儿的琳琅满目岂是我敢——奢望——

我从未品尝过这样的美味——
它跟我和鸟儿在大自然的
餐间里经常共享的碎屑
有着天壤之别——

这丰盛刺伤了我——我还不太习惯——
它叫我有些不适——有些陌生感——
就像山间灌木丛里的——浆果——
倏然被移植到了——马路边——

我不再觉得饿了——于是我发现
饥饿——只是立在橱窗外面的人
所持有的一种感觉——
一旦进到里面——它便立刻消散——

I had been hungry, all the Years —
My Noon had Come — to dine —
I trembling drew the Table near —
And touched the Curious Wine —

'Twas this on Tables I had seen —
When turning, hungry, Home
I looked in Windows, for the Wealth
I could not hope — for Mine —

I did not know the ample Bread —
'Twas so unlike the Crumb
The Birds and I, had often shared
In Nature's — Dining Room —

The Plenty hurt me — 'twas so new —
Myself felt ill — and odd —
As Berry — of a Mountain Bush —
Transplanted — to a Road —

Nor was I hungry — so I found
That Hunger — was a way
Of Persons outside Windows —
The Entering — takes away —

生与死的启示

Life & Death

我思忖（NO.301）

我思忖，地球有大限——
痛苦——无边无沿——
许多人受到了伤害，
可是，那又怎么样呢？

我思忖，我们会死去
最强健的生命力
也不能不被消蚀，
可是，那又怎么样呢？

我思忖，在天堂——
抑或能得到些许的补偿——
会有一种新的景象——
可是，那又怎么样呢？

I reason, Earth is short —

And Anguish — absolute —

And many hurt,

But, what of that?

I reason, we could die —

The best Vitality

Cannot excel Decay,

But, what of that?

I reason, that in Heaven —

Somehow, it will be even —

Some new Equation, given —

But, what of that?

我为美而死（NO.449）

我为美而死——当我
刚被安顿到坟茔里
为真理而死的那一位，便把
声音从隔壁的屋里——

轻轻地传过来：“为啥而死？”
“为美”，我回答说——
“我——为真理——它们是一回事——
我们是兄妹了，”他说——

于是像一对亲人在夜里相遇——
我们隔着屋子谈天谈地——
直到藓苔蔓上了我们的唇边——
掩盖了——我们的姓氏——

I died for Beauty — but was scarce
Adjusted in the Tomb
When One who died for Truth, was lain
In an adjoining room —

He questioned softly "Why I failed"?
"For Beauty", I replied —
"And I — for Truth — Themself are One —
We Brethren, are", He said —

And so, as Kinsmen, met a Night —
We talked between the Rooms —
Until the Moss had reached our lips —
And covered up — our names —

我们只是见过启航（NO.43）

活——真能算活——
死——真能算死——
人的笑颜真能
凭着其对生人的信任
把心灵禀陈？

真能离开自己熟悉的地域
奔赴一个人烟稀少的地方
真能在筹划这一旅行时
心里没有丝毫的彷徨？

有人禀有这样一种信任，
但不是在我们这个年代——
我们只是见到过启航
可自己从未航过海！

Could live — did live —

Could die — did die —

Could smile upon the whole

Through faith in one he met not,

To introduce his soul.

Could go from scene familiar

To an untraversed spot —

Could contemplate the journey

With unpuzzled heart —

Such trust had one among us,

Among us not today —

We who saw the launching

Never sailed the Bay!

如果（NO.56）

如果在过节的时候
我不再带来玫瑰，
那是因为我已到了阴间
远离了玫瑰——

如果对我的那些可爱的蓓蕾
我不再把它们的名字使用——
那是因为死神的手指
已捏住了我翕动的嘴唇！

If I should cease to bring a Rose
Upon a festal day,
'Twill be because beyond the Rose
I have been called away —

If I should cease to take the names
My buds commemorate —
'Twill be because Death's finger
Claps my murmuring lip!

如果这就是凋残（NO.120）

如果这就是“凋残”
哦，让我现在就变得“老衰”！
如果这就是“死亡”
请把我裹在这红色锦缎[①]里葬埋！
如果这就是“安眠”，
在这样美丽的夜晚
阖上眼该会有多么的骄傲！
傍晚好，亲爱的乡亲们！
孔雀想要离去了！

① 指夕照时的晚霞，这里有“夕阳无限好”之意。

If this is "fading"

Oh let me immediately "fade"!

If this is "dying"

Bury me, in such a shroud of red!

If this is "sleep,"

On such a night

How proud to shut the eye!

Good Evening, gentle Fellow men!

Peacock presumes to die!

当知更鸟飞来时（NO.182）

当知更鸟飞来时
如果我不再活着，
请代我给那只头上长红羽的鸟儿
一把食以示纪念。

如果我因睡得太死，
不能对你表示谢意，
你也要知道我的已像石头一样的
嘴唇一直在试着谢你！

If I shouldn't be alive
When the Robins come,
Give the one in Red Cravat,
A Memorial crumb.

If I couldn't thank you,
Being fast asleep,
You will know I'm trying
Why my Granite lip!

斜光（NO.258）

太阳斜照的余辉
于冬日的下午里——
就像教堂的音乐那般
给人以压抑——

它给我们的伤害，非属人为——
我们无由找到伤痕，
只是于内心里增添了
一种别样的情蕴——

没有谁能将它传授——
这一绝望感只能意会——
是上天凭借大气
将我们打击——

这光斜照时，大地在倾听——
影子——屏住了呼吸——
斜光消逝后，远近
都像罩上了死气——

There's a certain Slant of light,
Winter Afternoons —
That oppresses, like the Heft
Of Cathedral Tunes —

Heavenly Hurt, it gives us —
We can find no scar,
But internal difference,
Where the Meanings, are —

None may teach it — Any —
'Tis the Seal Despair —
An imperial affliction
Sent us of the Air —

When it comes, the Landscape listens —
Shadows — hold their breath —
When it goes, 'tis like the Distance
On the look of Death —

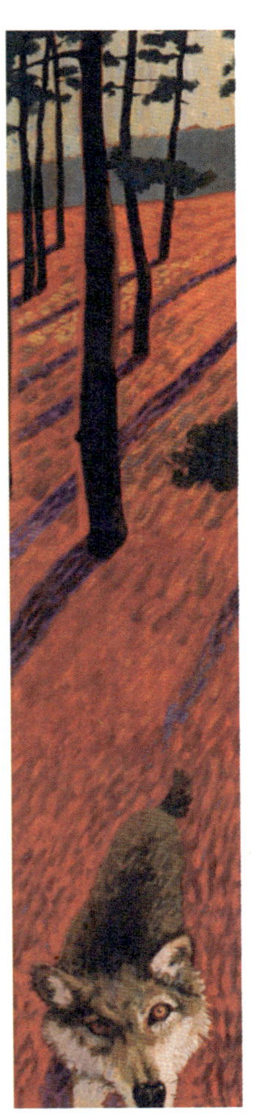

我，体验了葬礼（NO.280）

我于脑中，体验了我的葬礼，
吊唁的人来来往往
他们的脚步声响呀——响呀——直到
我的感官好像开裂了一样——

待他们都坐定以后，
如锣鼓般的祈祷声——
开始不停地回荡——回荡——直到我以为
我的头脑就要麻木不醒——

后来我听见他们抬起棺材，
带钉子的皮靴声于是
又在我的心头咔嚓咔嚓地碾过，
同时丧钟——也开始响起，

好像整个天宇都成了一口大钟，
人，只剩下耳朵在听，
于是我，寂静，还有那些陌生的种族
遭了殃，在这儿冷清——

末了理智的木板，一下子断开，
我往下掉落，掉落——
左冲右撞地摔到了底儿，
然后——我失去了知觉——

I felt a Funeral, in my Brain,
And Mourners to and fro
Kept treading — treading — till it seemed
That Sense was breaking through —

And when they all were seated,
A Service, like a Drum —
Kept beating — beating — till I thought
My Mind was going numb —

And then I heard them lift a Box
And creak across my Soul
With those same Boots of Lead, again,
Then Space — began to toll,

As all the Heavens were a Bell,

And Being, but an Ear,

And I, and Silence, some strange Race

Wrecked, solitary, here —

And then a Plank in Reason, broke,

And I dropped down, and down —

And hit a World, at every plunge,

And Finished knowing — then —

别样的欣然（NO.294）

要入黄泉的人——看着日出
有种别样的欣然——
因为——当朝霞再次燃起
他们还不知能否看见——

明天——就要死去的人
期盼聆听鸟儿的啁啾——
因为鸟的歌声会唤醒操着
他生杀大权的刀斧——

他们快乐——因为日出先于
他们的死期来到——
他们快乐——因为草原上的鸟儿带给
他们挽歌的曲调！

The Doomed — regard the Sunrise
With different Delight —
Because — when next it burns abroad
They doubt to witness it —

The Man — to die — tomorrow —
Harks for the Meadow Bird —
Because its Music stirs the Axe
That clamors for his head —

Joyful — to whom the Sunrise
Precedes Enamored — Day —
Joyful — for whom the Meadow Bird
Has ought but Elegy!

是生存给我们更多的伤痛（NO.335）

并不是死亡在深深地伤害我们——
是生存——给我们以更多的伤痛——
而死则——不同——
它是在门后面进行的那一种——

从南方飞来的鸟儿——习惯在——
霜露到来之前飞走——
去往更和暖的地方——
而我们却是那种宁要留下来过冬的鸟。

我们像是抖瑟地站在农夫的房门前——
硬要人家施舍点儿剩饭的可怜虫——
直到——怜悯我们的雪花
敦劝我们返回家中。

'Tis not that Dying hurts us so —
'Tis Living — hurts us more —
But Dying — is a different way —
A Kind behind the Door —

The Southern Custom — of the Bird —
That ere the Frosts are due —
Accepts a better Latitude —
We — are the Birds — that stay.

The Shrivers round Farmers' doors —
For whose reluctant Crumb —
We stipulate — till pitying Snows
Persuade our Feathers Home.

生命逝去时（NO.369）

她嬉玩似的躺在那里
她的生命已经逝去——
仿佛想着还要归来——
只是不会那么快——

她的胳膊闲适地耷拉着——
好像是因为运动的乏味——
一时间忘记了
再将它们抬起——

她未合上的眼睛还映着——光儿——
仿佛其主人仍然有着
灵感的火花——想要
把你——取笑——

停在她门前的晨光——
正企图，我想，
诱哄着她一直睡下去
睡得那么轻——又那么香——

She lay as if at play
Her life had leaped away —
Intending to return —
But not so soon —

Her merry Arms, half dropt —
As if for lull of sport —
An instant had forgot —
The Trick to start —

Her dancing Eyes — ajar —
As if their Owner were
Still sparkling through
For fun — at you —

Her Morning at the door —
Devising, I am sure —
To force her sleep —
So light — so deep —

从不延误的精灵（NO.390）

它来了——这个从不延误的精灵[①]
它走近了邻里——现在——走到了门口——
从其他所有的门栓中，它选定了门扣——
一边进到屋里一边问道：“先生，你认识我吗？”

很简单的行礼——心照不宣的辨识——
如说它是敌人它很勇敢，如说是朋友它很干练
给每个房间都挂起黑纱——
然后带魂儿出了屋子——去把上帝谒见——

① 指死神。

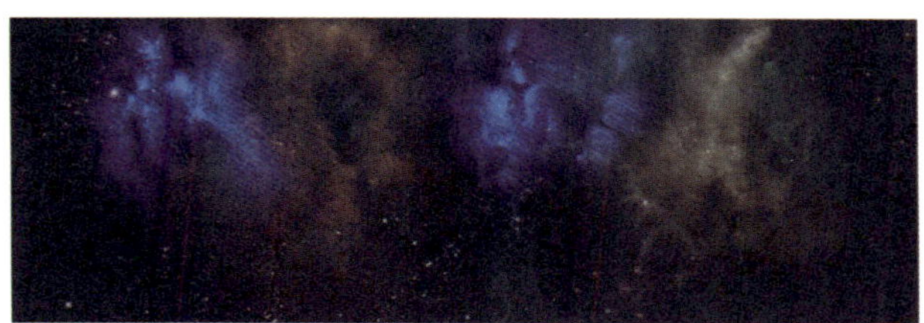

It's coming — the postponeless Creature —
It gains the Block — and now — it gains the Door —
Chooses its latch, from all the other fastenings —
Enters — with a "You know Me — Sir"?

Simple Salute — and certain Recognition —
Bold — were it Enemy — Brief — were it friend —
Dresses each House in Crape, and Icicle —
And carries one — out of it — to God —

我们离开得很远（NO.407）

我们不在坟头上玩耍
因为那儿没有空间——
而且——也不平——呈坡状——
人们前来吊唁

把花儿搁在坟上
拉着长长的脸——
我们担心他们的心儿就要坠下
把我们玩的兴致砸扁——

所以我们离开得很远
像躲开敌人那般——
有时回头只是为了知道我们
是否走得——足够的远——

We do not play on Graves —
Because there isn't Room —
Besides — it isn't even — it slants
And People come —

And put a Flower on it —
And hang their faces so —
We're fearing that their Hearts will drop —
And crush our pretty play —

And so we move as far
As Enemies — away —
Just looking round to see how far
It is — Occasionally —

爱的劳作（NO.478）

我没有时间去忌恨——

因为

墓穴到头来会阻止了我——

而且生命又很短促

不能容我

将敌意——长久地贯彻——

我也没有时间去爱——

不过既然

人生总得有所为——

一点爱的劳作

我想

于我已经足矣——

I had no time to Hate —

Because

The Grave would hinder Me —

And Life was not so

Ample I

Could finish — Enmity —

Nor had I time to Love —

But since

Some Industry must be —

The little Toil of Love —

I thought

Be large enough for Me —

我们一直陪伴你（NO.482）

我们盖上了你的——亲切的面庞——
不是因为我们厌倦了你——
是因为你自己已被我们弄得疲惫——
你可否记得——在你离去时——

我们一直陪伴你直到
你不再——把我们留意——
只是在那时我们才不情愿地扭转身子
把你在心里一遍遍地默记——

一边自责我们以前怎么会满足于
对你所施的那一点儿爱——
要是你现在——能够接受——
我们会给予你百般的温存——成倍的爱意——

We Cover Thee — Sweet Face —

Not that We tire of Thee —

But that Thyself fatigue of Us —

Remember — as Thou go —

We follow Thee until

Thou notice Us — no more —

And then — reluctant — turn away

To Con Thee o'er and o'er —

And blame the scanty love

We were Content to show —

Augmented — Sweet — a Hundred fold —

If Thou would'st take it — now —

只是这是事实（NO.566）

一只快要死去的老虎——呻吟着要水喝——
我寻遍了沙滩——
接住一些从石缝中渗下的水滴
用手捧着往回赶——

他硕大的眼珠——在死后显得滞重——
可是细看——在他的视网膜上——
我仍能看到
我和水的——映像——

这不能怪我——跑回得太慢——
也不能怪他——在我
为他送回水之前死去——
只是这是事实——他已经死了——

A Dying Tiger — moaned for Drink —
I hunted all the Sand —
I caught the Dripping of a Rock
And bore it in my Hand —

His Mighty Balls — in death were thick —
But searching — I could see
A Vision on the Retina
Of Water — and of me —

'Twas not my blame — who sped too slow —
'Twas not his blame — who died
While I was reaching him —
But 'twas — the fact that He was dead —

它们一直把我们等候（NO.607）

在一些特殊的场合灵魂能接近到
与她[1]早已割离的人和事——
那时朦胧——反倒显得古怪——
清晰——反倒变得——容易——

我们已埋葬掉的形体[2]就起居
在我们的周围，就好像在屋子里——
坟茔并没有能完全枯槁了他们的形容，
过去一同玩耍的伙伴返了回来——

他就身着他入殓时
穿的那件夹克
我们——从儿时就一起——玩耍——
后来——被阴阳两界分隔——

① 代指灵魂。
② 这里指已故的人。

墓穴交回了它夺去的东西——
我们共处过的欢乐岁月——
那些骨节上闪着光熠的精灵
用它们的羽翼向我们致敬——

当我们——也谢世的时候——
是它们[1]——一直在把我们等候——
是它们，而不是我们自己
在吊唁痛苦。

① 指精灵。

Of nearness to her sundered Things
The Soul has special times —
When Dimness — looks the Oddity —
Distinctness — easy — seems —

The Shapes we buried, dwell about,
Familiar, in the Rooms —
Untarnished by the Sepulchre,
The Mouldering Playmate comes —

In just the Jacket that he wore —
Long buttoned in the Mold
Since we — old mornings, Children — played —
Divided — by a world —

The Grave yields back her Robberies —

The Years, our pilfered Things —

Bright Knots of Apparitions

Salute us, with their wings —

As we — it were — that perished —

Themself — had just remained till we rejoin them —

And 'twas they, and not ourself

That mourned.

我会来到你的身边（NO.648）

我发誓——在你临死的时刻——
我会来到你的身边——
最后的悼念将是由我为你来做——
我会为你阖上眼睑——

不是用钱币——尽管它们能从一个帝王的
手中造出无数——
是用我的嘴唇——这正是你
未闭上的眼睛的要求——

当人们都离去以后——我仍会留下——
如果生命只是昙花一现脆弱得很
那就请上天再设造一次
使我得到——再生——

我整个生命的祭酒——会这样为你泼洒——
你若地下有知你便能看见
在对你的模仿中——生的福祚
做着对死的福祚的颂赞——

我会流连于你的坟旁
诱使太阳长时间地
在你的坟头——徜徉
喝令清晨的露滴

在你这边多多地聚集
以免好妒忌的青草
更鲜绿——更欣然地
簇拥在别人的坟头

我要追循你的音容笑貌，高风亮节——
永远不落得很远——
因为我要进的
天堂之门——
不是早已把我——拒绝在外面？

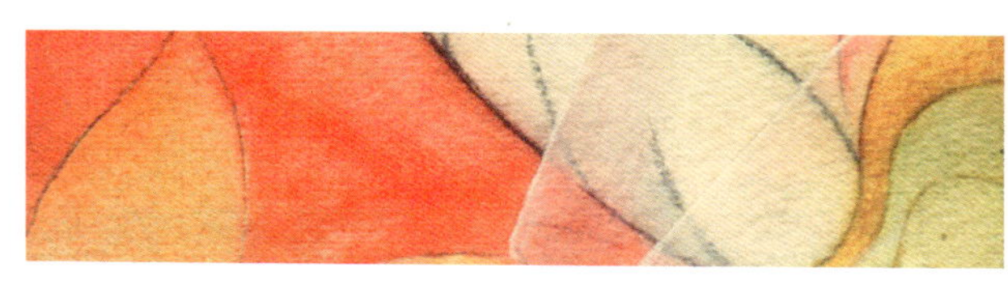

Promise This — When You be Dying —
Some shall summon Me —
Mine belong Your latest Sighing —
Mine — to Belt Your Eye —

Not with Coins — though they be Minted
From an Emperor's Hand —
Be my lips — the only Buckle
Your low Eyes — demand —

Mine to stay — when all have wandered —
To devise once more
If the Life be too surrendered —
Life of Mine — restore —

Poured like this — My Whole Libation —
Just that You should see
Bliss of Death — Life's Bliss extol thro'
Imitating You —

Mine — to guard Your Narrow Precinct —
To seduce the Sun
Longest on Your South, to linger,
Largest Dews of Morn

To demand, in Your low favor
Lest the Jealous Grass
Greener lean — Or fonder cluster
Round some other face —

Mine to supplicate Madonna —
If Madonna be
Could behold so far a Creature —
Christ — omitted — Me —

Just to follow Your dear future —
Ne'er so far behind —
For My Heaven —
Had I not been
Most enough — denied?

世间的帝王（NO.674）

有宾朋于家的灵魂
很少再外出——
至友至交的聚集在座——
将这种需求祛除——

而且礼节也阻止
主人的离去当
前来造访他的
是世间的帝王——

The Soul that hath a Guest
Doth seldom go abroad —
Diviner Crowd at Home —
Obliterate the need —

And Courtesy forbid
A Host's departure when
Upon Himself be visiting
The Emperor of Men —

还有永恒同在（NO.712）

因为我不能停下来等上死亡——
死亡便友好地为我停住车驾——
车上只坐着我们两个
还有永恒同在。

我们缓缓地前行——他不懂得匆忙——
我也摈弃掉
我的劳作连同悠闲，
以把他的好心回报。

我们经过了学校，那里的孩子们正在游戏
围成一个圈子——在操场上——
我们经过丰收在望的田野——
经过正在落下的太阳——

或者说——是太阳经过了我们——
露水使得我发冷和战栗——
因为我的衣服，只是薄纱——
我的披肩——只是网绢——

我们停在了一座房子前，
它好像只是——隆起的地块——
屋顶也看不太清楚——
屋檐——没在土里——

自那以后——已过去了几个世纪——
可我觉得那一天[①]比几个世纪还长
于是我第一次猜到那驾辕的马头
是朝着永恒的方向——

① 指诗中的“我”死去的那一天。

Because I could not stop for Death —
He kindly stopped for me —
The Carriage held but just Ourselves —
And Immortality.

We slowly drove — He knew no haste
And I had put away
My labor and my leisure too,
For His Civility —

We passed the School, where Children strove
At Recess — in the Ring —
We passed the Fields of Gazing Grain —
We passed the Setting Sun —

Or rather — He passed Us —
The Dews drew quivering and chill —
For only Gossamer, my Gown —
My Tippet — only Tulle —

We paused before a House that seemed
A Swelling of the Ground —
The Roof was scarcely visible —
The Cornice — in the Ground —

Since then — 'tis Centuries — and yet
Feels shorter than the Day
I first surmised the Horses' Heads
Were toward Eternity —

邀死亡莅临的人 · 无韵诗（NO.759）

他战斗像那些再没有什么可失去的人——
把自己置身于枪林弹雨
宛如一个觉得他以后的
生命已经无用——

而大胆邀死亡莅临的人——
可是死神却羞怯于他
恰如有的人对死神畏怯——
在他而言——活着——是负重——

他的同志们，像狂风吹舞下的雪片
被死神席卷而去——
可他——却因为渴求死亡
而存活下来——

He fought like those Who've nought to lose —
Bestowed Himself to Balls
As One who for a further Life
Had not a further Use —

Invited Death — with bold attempt —
But Death was Coy of Him
As Other Men, were Coy of Death —
To Him — to live — was Doom —

His Comrades, shifted like the Flakes
When Gusts reverse the Snow —
But He — was left alive Because
Of Greediness to die —

从空旷到空旷 · 无韵诗（NO.761）

从空旷到空旷——
沿着一条无任何线索可觅的路
我迈着机械的脚步——
或者停下——或者死去——或者前进——
在我都是一样——

即使我达到了目的
即使远方的目标
已在一个个地显露——
我仍然会闭上眼睛——摸索着走
盲目的行进——会轻松得多——

From Blank to Blank —
A Threadless Way
I pushed Mechanic feet —
To stop — or perish — or advance —
Alike indifferent —

If end I gained
It ends beyond
Indefinite disclosed —
I shut my eyes — and groped as well
'Twas lighter — to be Blind —

可爱的姑娘（NO.908）

太阳升起来了——可爱的姑娘——
你在白天里难道没有岗位？
迟迟不至，这可不是你一贯的作为——
勤劳的你快动起来——

已经是中午了——我可爱的姑娘
哦——你是不是还在睡觉？
百合花——在等待着你这新娘——
还有蜜蜂——难道你已把它们忘掉？

我可爱的姑娘——现在已是晚上——哦
夜晚才该属于你
而不是早晨——你是否已将你要
死去的消息昭示——
亲爱的，如果我当时不能劝说你回头，
我会帮助你——就此事[①]

① 指死去这件事。

'Tis Sunrise — Little Maid — Hast Thou
No Station in the Day?
'Twas not thy wont, to hinder so —
Retrieve thine industry —

'Tis Noon — My little Maid —
Alas — and art thou sleeping yet?
The Lily — waiting to be Wed —
The Bee — Hast thou forgot?

My little Maid — 'Tis Night — Alas
That Night should be to thee
Instead of Morning — Had'st thou broached
Thy little Plan to Die —
Dissuade thee, if I could not, Sweet,
I might have aided — thee —

我们与死者的距离（NO.949）

在光的下面，啊还要再下，
在青草和泥土的下面，
在甲虫的洞穴和
三叶草的根的下面，

哪怕是巨人的臂膀
也够不着
哪怕整年都是白昼的阳光
也照射不到，

在光之上，啊还要上，
在飞鸟之上——
在彗星的烟柱和——
最长的腕尺的丈量之上，

其远连猜想也不能跨越
连谜语也不能囊括——
噢，谁能划出我们与
死者间的距离相隔！

Under the Light, yet under,
Under the Grass and the Dirt,
Under the Beetle's Cellar
Under the Clover's Root,

Further than Arm could stretch
Were it Giant long,
Further than Sunshine could
Were the Day Year long,

Over the Light, yet over,
Over the Arc of the Bird —
Over the Comet's chimney —
Over the Cubit's Head,

Further than Guess can gallop
Further than Riddle ride —
Oh for a Disc to the Distance
Between Ourselves and the Dead!

我们将走过而不做诀别（NO.996）

我们将走过而不做诀别
这样便省去了
张人已不在了的证书——
以为在我

跟她生前分开的地方还能再找到她
只要我去找寻——
用这一方法，我避开了对死者的
思念之痛。

We'll pass without the parting
So to spare
Certificate of Absence —
Deeming where

I left Her I could find Her
If I tried —
This way, I keep from missing
Those that died.

韶光（NO.895）

一团云彩从天空褪去
霎时间韶光无限
不过这云这光已在
我脑中永远消散

倘若我当时再多眺望一会
倘若我当时把那荣光攫取
这一美好的记忆现在
会给我多大的助益。

在我于天堂站牢之前
我再不会轻易地一瞥一点头
就从天使身旁走过
这就是我现在的念头。

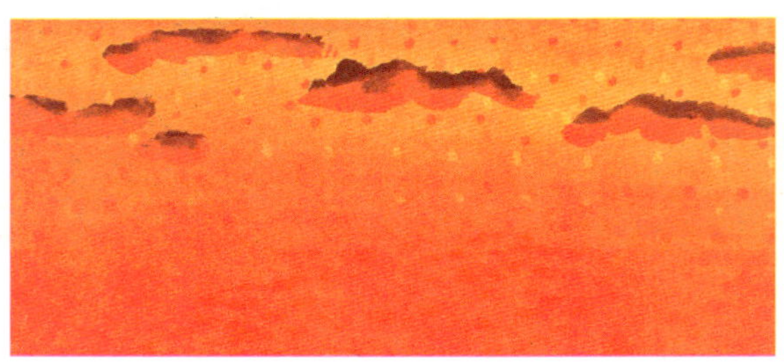

A Cloud withdrew from the Sky
Superior Glory be
But that Cloud and its Auxiliaries
Are forever lost to me

Had I but further scanned
Had I secured the Glow
In an Hermetic Memory
It had availed me now.

Never to pass the Angel
With a glance and a Bow
Till I am firm in Heaven
Is my intention now.

奇迹（NO.1017）

死去了——仍然活着
活着——却已经死去
这一充满嘲讽意味的“奇迹”
对“相信”提出了质疑

To die — without the Dying
And live — without the Life
This is the hardest Miracle
Propounded to Belief.

生命的可贵（NO.1741）

生命不能失而复得
这使生命显得尤为可贵。
硬去相信我们不相信的东西
并不能给我们带来惊喜。

我们不妨打个比喻，说生命顶多
是一易耗尽的家资——
这往往激起一种逆反的欲望
叫生命更快地耗蚀。

That it will never come again
Is what makes life so sweet.
Believing what we don't believe
Does not exhilarate.

That if it be, it be at best
An ablative estate —
This instigates an appetite
Precisely opposite.

出于爱心（NO.1021）

出于爱心，我们的天父毋宁
常常带着其所选之子
跋涉在长满荆棘的荒野
而不是宜人的草地。

常常叫龙的粗利的爪
而不是朋友的手
引导着他抵达
要到的故土。

Far from Love the Heavenly Father
Leads the Chosen Child,
Oftener through Realm of Briar
Than the Meadow mild.

Oftener by the Claw of Dragon
Than the Hand of Friend
Guides the Little One predestined
To the Native Land.

弥留之际（NO.1026）

亲爱的，于弥留之际的人只需要很少，
有一杯清凉的水，
有一束颜色淡雅的花
挂饰在他的墙壁，足矣。

有一把扇子，或许，一个朋友的
遗憾和肯定，足矣；
在你离去时没有人会去注意
外面彩虹绚丽的色彩。

The Dying need but little, Dear,
A Glass of Water's all,
A Flower's unobtrusive Face
To punctuate the Wall,

A Fan, perhaps, a Friend's Regret
And Certainty that one
No color in the Rainbow
Perceive, when you are gone.

打开你的栅栏（NO.1065）

打开你的栅栏，噢死神——
让疲惫的羊群进来
它们的叫声已经停止
它们的徜徉已经终结——

你的夜晚最安静
你的栏圈最牢靠
你贴近得我们无需寻找
温柔得无以言表。

Let down the Bars, Oh Death —
The tired Flocks come in
Whose bleating ceases to repeat
Whose wandering is done —

Thine is the stillest night
Thine the securest Fold
Too near Thou art for seeking Thee
Too tender, to be told.

死亡之霜（NO.1136）

死亡之霜敷到了窗棂上——
他说“看好你的花儿”。
像海员拼命抢救漏水的船只一样
我们开始与死亡拼搏。

我们把无奈的花拿到海边——
拿到山上——和阳光底下
然而就是在他[①]那红彤彤的光束里
也有霜儿在卧爬——

我们把他[②]使劲地往后搡
将我们自己楔在

① 指太阳。
② 指霜。

他和花儿的中间，
可是像条细长的蛇一样
他很容易地就挤了过来
直到她的美丽无助地消亡
于是我们开始愤怒咆哮——
我们追猎他到他的山谷
我们跟踪他到他的老巢——

我们仇恨死亡仇恨生命
再也没有任何地方可去——
有一个比海洋和陆地还要
大的东西——那就是痛苦——

The Frost of Death was on the Pane —
"Secure your Flower" said he.
Like Sailors fighting with a Leak
We fought Mortality.

Our passive Flower we held to Sea —
To Mountain — To the Sun —
Yet even on his Scarlet shelf
To crawl the Frost begun —

We pried him back
Ourselves we wedged
Himself and her between,
Yet easy as the narrow Snake
He forked his way along

Till all her helpless beauty bent
And then our wrath begun —
We hunted him to his Ravine
We chased him to his Den —

We hated Death and hated Life
And nowhere was to go —
Than Sea and continent there is
A larger — it is Woe —

肃穆的大街（NO.1159）

肃穆的大街一直通向那——
万事已休止的近邻[①]——
那儿没有告示——没有异议
没有宇宙——没有法令——

看钟表，现在是早晨，可远处的
钟声却在召唤着黑夜——
已过去的年代在那里
没有根基。

① 指墓地。

Great Streets of silence led away
To Neighborhoods of Pause —
Here was no Notice — no Dissent
No Universe — no laws —

By Clocks, 'twas Morning, and for Night
The Bells at Distance called —
But Epoch had no basis here
For Period exhaled.

那一刺痛（NO.1272）

她那么愿意骄傲地死去
使我们都感到了羞辱
我们所憧憬的，与她的心愿
似乎显得格格不入——

她那么乐于即刻去到
我们都不想去的地域
以致我们所感到的那一刺痛
几近于变成了嫉妒——

So proud she was to die
It made us all ashamed
That what we cherished, so unknown
To her desire seemed —

So satisfied to go
Where none of us should be
Immediately — that Anguish stooped
Almost to Jealousy —

我了解你更深（NO.1666）

我看你更清楚因为有坟茔
挟着你的面颊
什么镜子也不能比那块碑石
把你照得更亮——

我了解你更深因为这
叫你不复存在的死亡
树梢上的空巢告诉我们
鸟儿已经离去到了它方。

I see thee clearer for the Grave
That took thy face between
No Mirror could illumine thee
Like that impassive stone —

I know thee better for the Act
That made thee first unknown
The stature of the empty nest
Attests the Bird that's gone.

她却要离去（NO.1703）

感觉一阵惬意，于她弥留之际的房间里
听到钟表生动的嘀嗒声——
如果有风儿大胆地走近叩着门扉
也能给我们片刻的轻松——
外面孩子们的玩耍声可把思绪
从死的主题挪开——
可是这会叫我们觉得更糟
因为他们都活着
而她却要离去了。

‘Twas comfort in her Dying Room
To hear the living Clock —
A short relief to have the wind
Walk boldly up and knock —
Diversion from the Dying Theme
To hear the children play —
But wrong the more
That these could live
And this of ours must die.

她悄然地去了（NO.149）

她悄然地去了，就像露珠
在清晨过后从花枝上逝去。
与露水不同的是，她在夜凉时
没再能把脸露！

像一颗星星那样她轻轻地在我的
夏日生活开始时陨落了——
想到她没有勒威耶[①]的老练
令我备受熬煎！

① 法国天文学家，1811年—1877年，用数学方法推算出那时尚未出现的海王星的位置。

She went as quiet as the Dew
From an Accustomed flower.
Not like the Dew, did she return
At the Accustomed hour!

She dropt as softly as a star
From out my summer's Eve —
Less skillful than Le Verriere
It's sorer to believe!

我还没有告诉我的花园（NO.50）

我还没有告诉我的花园——
免得我无法控制自己的感情。
我还没有足够的勇气
现在就把它告诉蜜蜂——

我不会在街上把它传布
那样店铺的门面都会拿眼把我瞪
这么腼腆——这么无知的一个人
竟敢直面死神。

也不能让山丘得知这一消息——
在那里我曾漫步多少次——
也不能告诉可爱的树林
我要走的那个日子——

在饭桌上也不要吐露——
不能一不留神
对别人暗示出有人
今天将要步入“迷宫”[①]。

① 原文是大写的“Riddle”，这儿指阴间地府。

I haven't told my garden yet —
Lest that should conquer me.
I haven't quite the strength now
To break it to the Bee —

I will not name it in the street
For shops would stare at me —
That one so shy — so ignorant
Should have the face to die.

The hillsides must not know it —
Where I have rambled so —
Nor tell the loving forests
The day that I shall go —

Nor lisp it at the table —
Nor heedless by the way
Hint that within the Riddle
One will walk today —

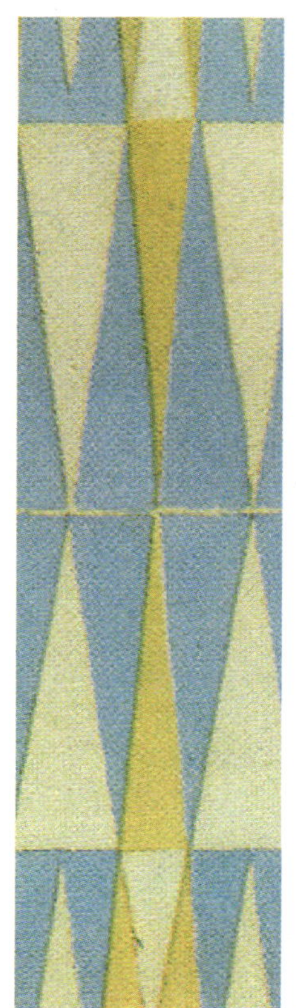

灵魂的自由
Freedom of Soul

灵魂选择自己的伴侣（NO.56）

灵魂选择好自己的伴侣——
然后——关闭了窗门——
对其他崇美的人和物
再也不眷顾操心——

高马轩车——停在——她寒伧的门前——
她不为所动——
皇帝君王——跪坐在她的陋席上面
她不为所动——

我知道她从一个富裕的民族——
选好其所要——
然后——关闭了她的心府——
像石头再不受侵扰——

The Soul selects her own Society —
Then — shuts the Door —
To her divine Majority —
Present no more —

Unmoved — she notes the Chariots — pausing —
At her low Gate —
Unmoved — an Emperor be kneeling
Upon her Mat —

I've known her — from an ample nation —
Choose One —
Then — close the Valves of her attention —
Like Stone —

我的灵魂拥有自由（NO.384）

任何痛苦也不能使我屈服——
我的灵魂——拥有自由——
在这一可折可朽的骨架背后
还有钢筋铁骨铸就——

你用锯不能穿透——
弯刀也不能刺入——
所以——有两个身体——
一个在飞翔——个在羁缚——

巢里的鹰可以
自如地离开——
又自如地飞上蓝天
你也可以完全这般——

除非是你自己
成了你的敌人——
是否受缚决定于意识
自由亦然。

No Rack can torture me —
My Soul — at Liberty —
Behind this mortal Bone
There knits a bolder One —

You cannot prick with saw —
Nor pierce with Scimitar —
Two Bodies — therefore be —
Bind One — The Other fly —

The Eagle of his Nest
No easier divest —
And gain the Sky
Than mayest Thou —

Except Thyself may be
Thine Enemy —
Captivity is Consciousness —
So's Liberty.

不要让灵魂感到乏味（NO.1430）

从未有过憧憬的人——就还
没有体味了狂喜——
节制的饮食会使丰盛的
酒宴也黯淡无辉——

希冀和目标应订在心智能够到的范围
尽管还没有被抓到手里——
不要靠得再近——以免“现实”
叫你的灵魂感到了乏味

Who never wanted — maddest Joy
Remains to him unknown —
The Banquet of Abstemiousness
Defaces that of Wine —

Within its reach, though yet ungrasped
Desire's perfect Goal —
No nearer — lest the Actual —
Should disentrall thy soul —

灵魂的倦怠（NO.396）

对于生命，倦怠比痛苦
更能切入肌肤——
它是痛苦的后嗣——来自灵魂
已尝尽了痛苦之后——

一种困顿感——弥漫着——
一种似雾的朦胧模糊
将意识团团围起——
像大雾把巉岩罩住。

手术大夫不会看到——痛苦而变色——
他练就了——这种本事——
可是如若告诉他那个躺着的人
其感觉已经停止——

他会告诉你——手术已为时太晚——
一个比他强大的力量——
在他之前发生了作用——
那儿的生命力已经消亡。

There is a Languor of the Life
More imminent than Pain —
'Tis Pain's Successor — When the Soul
Has suffered all it can —

A Drowsiness — diffuses —
A Dimness like a Fog
Envelops Consciousness —
As Mists — obliterate a Crag.

The Surgeon — does not blanch — at pain
His Habit — is severe —
But tell him that it ceased to feel —
The Creature lying there —

And he will tell you — skill is late —
A Mightier than He —
Has ministered before Him —
There's no Vitality.

真谛（NO.306）

灵魂升至极境的情形
只在她一个人身上发生——
那时朋友——和人世的纷扰
都会无限邈远地退隐——

或者说她——自己——升到了
一个遥不可及的高度
以至除了她的上帝
谁也认她不出——

这一对世俗的完全忘却
极为少见——可像精灵
一样的美好——像空气
一样的轻盈——

永恒只对一些
精英们——揭示——
其浩瀚不朽的
真谛。

The Soul's Superior instants
Occur to Her — alone —
When friend — and Earth's occasion
Have infinite withdrawn —

Or She — Herself — ascended
To too remote a Height
For lower Recognition
Than Her Omnipotent —

This Mortal Abolition
Is seldom — but as fair
As Apparition — subject
To Autocratic Air —

Eternity's disclosure
To favorites — a few —
Of the Colossal substance

庇护（NO.578）

外面的身体生长得
很是自如和适宜——
如果灵魂——想要躲藏
它[①]的殿堂总是稳稳而立，

半开着门扉——邀灵魂进来——
它从来也不背弃庄重
肃穆地恳求要在它里面
庇护的灵魂

① 指身体。

The Body grows without —
The more convenient way —
That if the Spirit — like to hide
Its Temple stands, alway,

Ajar — secure — inviting —
It never did betray
The Soul that asked its shelter
In solemn honesty

一个人不必做宅所（NO.670）

一个人不必做有幽灵萦绕的——屋子——
一个人不必做宅所——
他的大脑里就有弯弯曲曲的通廊，胜于
某一有形的处所——

在深夜里遇到一个可见的鬼
远比在它[①]的内壳
与其冷静的主人面对——
安全得多。

奔走在教堂的墓地
追逐鬼的魂魄——
也远比孑然一身，毫无戒备时——
与自我相对安全得多——

藏匿在我们自己——后面的自我——
往往会把我们惊得目瞪口呆——
而伏在我们家里的窃贼
倒会叫我们觉得是最小的惊骇。

身体——借了一支左轮手枪——
并将门闩插妥
可却忽略了至上的精灵——
乃至更多——

① 指大脑。

One need not be a Chamber — to be Haunted —

One need not be a House —

The Brain has Corridors — surpassing

Material Place —

Far safer, of a Midnight Meeting

External Ghost

Than its interior Confronting —

That Cooler Host.

Far safer, through an Abbey gallop,

The Stones a'chase —

Than Unarmed, one's a'self encounter —

In lonesome Place —

Ourself behind ourself, concealed —

Should startle most —

Assassin hid in our Apartment

Be Horror's least.

The Body — borrows a Revolver —

He bolts the Door —

O'erlooking a superior spectre —

Or More —

灵魂的载体（NO.751）

我所有的怀疑都与我自己的价值有关——
我所有的不安——是他[①]的功德——
与其相比，我的品质
显得寒伧卑怯——

在我疑虑杂沓的头脑里
我最担心的莫过于——
我被证明我不能将
他高贵的需求满足——

① 指造物主或神明。

无庸置疑——神从内里
倾向于纡尊降贵——
因为其没有更高的
东西可以依藉——

我——这个不相匹的
他之选中的载体——
就这样宽慰着我的灵魂——就好像，
教堂愧对于在它里面做的祭礼——

My Worthiness is all my Doubt —
His Merit — all my fear —
Contrasting which, my quality
Do lowlier — appear —

Lest I should insufficient prove
For His beloved Need —
The Chiefest Apprehension
Upon my thronging Mind —

'Tis true — that Deity to stoop
Inherently incline —
For nothing higher than Itself
Itself can rest upon —

So I — the undivine abode
Of His Elect Content —
Conform my Soul — as 'twere a Church,
Unto Her Sacrament —

灵魂与不朽之间的联系（NO.974）

灵魂与不朽之间的联系
最显著地于
危险和突发的灾难中
得到揭示——

恰如闪电能在旷野上昭示出
我们未曾注意到的景观——
凭藉其快速的——闪光——
霹雳和发生的突然。

The Soul's distinct connection

With immortality

Is best disclosed by Danger

Or quick Calamity —

As Lightning on a Landscape

Exhibits Sheets of Place —

Not yet suspected — but for Flash —

And Click — and Suddenness.

尘封的灵魂（NO.1630）

就像轻气球向大地只恳求
将它放飞而别无所望——
它是为升腾而造就
它无定所地飞翔——
灵魂也愤愤然望着
尘封了它这么长时间的
泥土[①]
犹如小鸟
被人骗走了它的歌。

As from the earth the light Balloon
Asks nothing but release —
Ascension that for which it was,
Its soaring Residence.
The spirit looks upon the Dust
That fastened it so long
With indignation,
As a Bird
Defrauded of its song.

---

① 也有指肉体之意。

命运的门栓（NO.1523）

在我们动身时我们不知道这就是离去——
我们讪笑着关阖了门——
命运接踵而来在我们后面扣上了门闩——
我们再也无缘相逢——

We never know we go when we are going —
We jest and shut the Door —
Fate — following — behind us bolts it —
And we accost no more —

逃脱的生命（NO.1535）

羁缚太紧的生命一旦逃脱
就会迅跑再不停止
并且不时地回头顾盼着
有无缰绳的魔影相随——

闻到青草的香味、看到大草原上
草浪翻滚的马儿
只有用枪弹打中了它
才能将它再次捕获——

The Life that tied too tight escapes

Will ever after run

With a prudential look behind

And spectres of the Rein —

The Horse that scents the living Grass

And sees the Pastures smile

Will be retaken with a shot

If he is caught at all —

获得解放的心灵（NO.1587）

他咀嚼、畅饮着珍贵的言词——
他的精神变得强健——
他不再觉得自己贫穷，
不再感到肉体的存在——

他跳着舞打发这黯淡的时日
这一叫他长上了翅膀的馈赠
只是一本书——噢，能带来多大的自由
一个获得解放的心灵——

He ate and drank the precious Words —
His Spirit grew robust —
He knew no more that he was poor,
Nor that his frame was Dust —

He danced along the dingy Days
And this Bequest of Wings
Was but a Book — What Liberty
A loosened spirit brings —

绳子与玉饰（NO.1322）

钗簪玉饰不能把你从深渊里救出
可是一条绳子会——
然而一条绳子作为纪念物
却又显得不那么雅致——

不过我要告诉你人生的每一步都是
一条濠沟——每一暂停处都是个陷阱——
现在你是要绳子还是玉饰?
如果它们的价钱也相近——

Floss won't save you from an Abyss
But a Rope will —
Notwithstanding a Rope for a Souvenir
Is not beautiful —

But I tell you every step is a Trough —
And every stop a Well —
Now will you have the Rope or the Floss?
Prices reasonable —

运气（NO.1350）

好运的降至并非偶然——

它是耕耘的结果——

运气昂贵的笑颜

是靠辛劳赢得——

财宝的祖先是那些

被我们嗤之以鼻的

古旧硬币

Luck is not chance —

It's Toil —

Fortune's expensive smile

Is earned —

The Father of the Mine

Is that old-fashioned Coin

We spurned —

希望（NO.1392）

希望是一种奇怪的发明
是心灵的专利——
一直在不停地行动
可从来也不疲惫——

对这一发着电火花的部件
我们还一无所知
但正是它的无与伦比的驱动力
点化着我们的一切——

Hope is a strange invention —
A Patent of the Heart —
In unremitting action
Yet never wearing out —

Of this electric Adjunct
Not anything is known
But its unique momentum
Embellish all we own —

渺小（NO.796）

有巨人做知己的，跟卑微的人在一起
会觉得局促和羞怯——
因为伟岸在渺小的一群中
会感到不自在——

而卑微的却不会被什么搅扰——
夏日的蚊虫扬扬自得地飞绕——
从没意识到它的掠过在天空里
显得多么渺小——

Who Giants know, with lesser Men
Are incomplete, and shy —
For Greatness, that is ill at ease
In minor Company —

A Smaller, could not be perturbed —
The Summer Gnat displays —
Unconscious that his single Fleet
Do not comprise the skies —

乖顺（NO.941）

女主人给她的小鸟喂食
次数很少——
小鸟没有怨言没有异议
只是乖顺地认识到

在主人的手和她自己的无食
还有荒远之地之间的鸿沟
因而跪下她那黄色的膝
俯身温顺地称慕——

The Lady feeds Her little Bird
At rarer intervals —
The little Bird would not dissent
But meekly recognize

The Gulf between the Hand and Her
And crumbless and afar
And fainting, on Her yellow Knee
Fall softly, and adore —

梦（NO.1376）

梦是奇妙的嫁妆
它让人们富足一段时光——
然后将我们从紫色的大门
抛出，一下子沦为“穷人”
重新回到以往
那——冷酷的现状——

Dreams are the subtle Dower
That make us rich an Hour —
Then fling us poor
Out of the purple Door
Into the Precinct raw
Possessed before —

光明（NO.1233）

如果我没有见过太阳
或许我能忍受了黑暗
可是光明已经煽起我新的欲念
使我不同于从前——

Had I not seen the Sun
I could have borne the shade
But Light a newer Wilderness
My Wilderness has made —

泥膏（NO.320）

我们把弄泥膏 [①]——
直至熟练到能制作珠宝——
那时，我们丢掉了泥膏——
认为我们自己很傻——

不过——它们的形状——很是相似——
我们笨拙的手
通过玩捏泥巴——
掌握了雕琢宝石的技术——

We play at Paste —
Till qualified, for Pearl —
Then, drop the Paste —
And deem ourself a fool —

The Shapes — though — were similar —
And our new Hands
Learned Gem-Tactics —
Practicing Sands —

① 制作假宝石的原料。

信心（NO.377）

人失掉信心——比损失了
财产更严重——
因为财产可以重新获得
信心不行——

信心与生俱来——
其生命——只有——一次
丢掉了它——
生活便犹如——乞食——

To lose one's faith — surpass
The loss of an Estate —
Because Estates can be
Replenished — faith cannot —

Inherited with Life —
Belief — but once — can be —
Annihilate a single clause —
And Being's — Beggary —

命运的短促（NO.857）

不稳定的租赁——给时间罩上
一层荣光
没把握的拥有，生发出对占有物的
倍加赞赏——

命运的短促——常常是最主要的
动因
说明了继承者们为什么对其所有
那么珍重——

Uncertain lease — develops lustre
On Time
Uncertain Grasp, appreciation
Of Sum —

The shorter Fate — is oftener the chiefest
Because
Inheritors upon a tenure
Prize —

魔鬼（NO.1479）

魔鬼——倘若他具有了忠诚的品质
就会是人们最好的朋友——
因为他有能力——
只是魔鬼不可能被挽救——
如若他不再背信弃义
他身上有的便都成了美德
魔鬼——毫无疑问
就会变得无比圣洁

The Devil — had he fidelity
Would be the best friend —
Because he has ability —
But Devils cannot mend —
Perfidy is the virtue
That would but he resign
The Devil — without question
Were thoroughly divine

天使就在隔壁（NO.1544）

在人世间没有找到天堂的——人们——
在天上也不会找到它——
因为天使就住在我们的隔壁，
不管我们往哪儿搬家——

Who has not found the Heaven — below —
Will fail of it above —
For Angels rent the House next ours,
Wherever we remove —

信念的失去（NO.1551）

那些——从前死去的人，
知道他们是去到哪里——
他们去到了上帝的右手那儿——
现在那只手被截掉了
上帝无处可觅了——

信念的失去
使我们的行为变得渺小——
纵便是一点磷火的光亮
也胜过完全没有光照——

Those — dying then,
Knew where they went —
They went to God's Right Hand —
That Hand is amputated now
And God cannot be found —

The abdication of Belief
Makes the Behavior small —
Better an ignis fatuus
Than no illume at all —

上帝的原因（NO.1163）

上帝做什么事情都有其原因，
造出每个心灵都有其目的，
我们的推断往往很不成熟，
我们推论的前提常常欠妥。

God made no act without a cause,
Nor heart without an aim,
Our inference is premature,
Our premises to blame.

裂痕 · 无韵诗（NO.546）

要补好裂痕
需嵌进引发了那一裂痕的因子
用别的
去充塞——只能使裂口开得更大——
你不能用空气将一道鸿沟
填平。

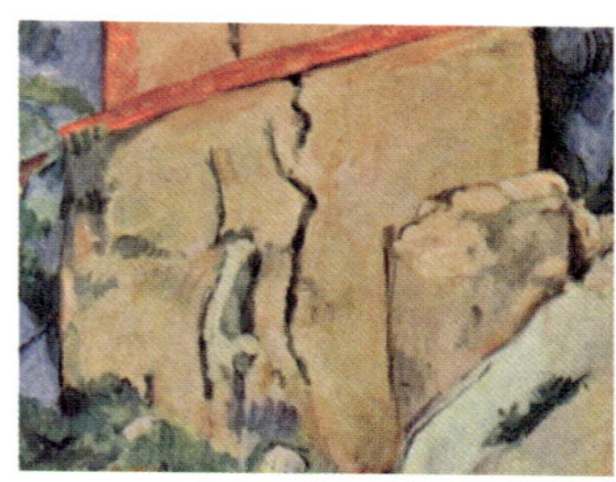

To fill a Gap
Insert the Thing that caused it —
Block it up
With Other — and 'twill yawn the more —
You cannot solder an Abyss
With Air.

昨天是个秘密（NO.1292）

昨天已成为历史
它已远远地离去——
昨天是史诗——
是哲学——

昨天是个秘密
站在今天的角度
在我们做着聪明的猜测时
两者[①]都已遁去

Yesterday is History,
'Tis so far away —
Yesterday is Poetry —
'Tis Philosophy —

Yesterday is mystery —
Where it is Today
While we shrewdly speculate
Flutter both away

① 指过去和现在。

消息（NO.1319）

消息在途中时会有怎样的感觉
如果消息也有心智
在降至到邻里时
它会像一支标枪冲进家里！

消息会如何做想
如果消息也能思忖
当它考虑到它那无形的负荷
有多么巨大惊人！

消息会怎么做当所有的人
都对它作同样的解释
当整个宇宙中不再有
一件要告诉的事？

How News must feel when travelling
If News have any Heart
Alighting at the Dwelling
'Twill enter like a Dart!

What News must think when pondering
If News have any Thought
Concerning the stupendousness
Of its perceiveless freight!

What News will do when every Man
Shall comprehend as one
And not in all the Universe
A thing to tell remain?

忘却（NO.1329）

他们是不是已经忘记了
或者正在忘掉
或者从来就不曾放在心上——
对此，还是不知道的好——

推测和猜想的苦恼
是一种较为温和的伤悲
比之于那——用“我知道”来加以强调的
铁一般的事实。

Whether they have forgotten
Or are forgetting now
Or never remembered —
Safer not to know —

Miseries of conjecture
Are a softer woe
Than a Fact of Iron
Hardened with I know —

附录一：生平年谱

艾米莉·狄金森（1830—1886年），美国女诗人，被视为二十世纪现代主义诗歌的先驱之一，与 华尔特·惠特曼被誉为美国诗歌星空中的“双子星”。一生创作诗歌1789首，生前仅发表了10首。

1830年12月10日，生于马萨诸塞州阿默斯特镇，父亲是该镇的首席律师，祖父是阿默斯特州学院的创始人，从小受到正统宗教教育，只在阿默斯特附近的一所女子学校读过一年书。

1835年9月，开始上小学。

1840年，全家搬离童年旧居；与妹妹一起进入安默斯特学院读书。

1844年，因表姐妹兼密友患斑疹伤寒症并最终死亡，感受到来自死亡“不断加深的威胁”，精神几近崩溃。

1847年8月，结束了安默斯特学院的学习，并进入位于南海德利的曼荷莲女子神学院。

1848年3月，兄弟奥斯丁将其带回家。

1850年，开始写诗。

1852年3月，文学导师、挚友、律师班哲明·法兰克林·牛顿去世。

1855年，与维妮拜访华盛顿特区、费城等地。

1855年11月，家族重购田产，搬回美因街的家宅，在房子里种植许多冬天能开花的植物，并且在窗户边小书桌上写过许多诗。

1856年，自制的面包在当地农业博览会的比赛中取得二等奖。

1858年，开始闭门不出（文学史中称其为“阿默斯特的女尼”）。

1860年，受到牧师查尔斯·魏兹华斯的拜访；出现精神激变，原因不详。

1861年，进入最富有创造力的时期，诗歌更具活力和激情，该年创作诗歌86首。

1862年4月，首次写信给汤玛斯·温沃·希金森；创作诗歌366首。

1863年，创作诗歌141首。

1864年，诗作刊登在《春田共和国报》；在剑桥求诊一位波士顿的眼科医师；创作诗歌174首。

1870年8月，到安贺斯特拜访艾米莉。

1873年12月3日，再度拜访艾米莉。

1874年6月16日，父亲爱德华·狄金森在波士顿去世。

1875年6月15日，母亲中风。

1878年11月20日，诗作在《成功》刊登；与父亲的朋友和同事、时年65岁的洛德法官恋爱，洛德法官曾经希望与艾米莉结婚，可是受到了拒绝。

1880年，魏兹华斯再度拜访。

1882年4月1日，魏兹华斯去世；11月14日，母亲去世。

1884年3月13日，洛德法官去世；写下一首以新娘自居而语涉“拥有”和“被拥有”的诗作《敬畏的新娘在你身边》，献给洛德表达对爱的追求。

1886年5月15日，死于肾脏疾病；

1886年5月19日，举行丧礼。

附录二：诗人的自白

1. 我从未如此享受完美的祥和与快乐，好像在这么短的时间里，我找到了我的救世主。

2. 非常高兴独自与上帝交谈，似乎上帝正在聆听我的祷告。

3. 有人坚持，在安息日去教堂做礼拜—；但是我却坚持，安息日在家中度过。

4. 当我还是小女孩时，我有一位朋友（牛顿），他教会了我不朽的精神，但是他自己却冒险太近了，以至于他再也没有回来。

5. 我安安静静地活着，只为了书册，因为没有一个舞台，能让我扮演自己的戏。不过思想本身就是自己的舞台，也定义着自己的存在。

6. 记录一个就等于同时记录另一个，就像将开得最美的鲜花夹在书页间一样。所以，让这个日记成为写给自己的信吧，这样就无需回信。

7. 诗就像是一绺金色的线穿过我的心，带领我往梦中才出现过的地方前进。我猜想我的字句并不能说明我的心，因为我的朋友们从来都不了解。

8. 我知道我的生命可以用来织这条线，它会变成一匹够亮的布，充满乐趣，也强韧到能抗拒焦虑；它是所有人的衣装。许多人都将生命托付给神，我却将我的生命托付给诗。

9. 信仰本身就是我们的十字架，我们在它的沉重下蹒跚前进，但却始终放不下它。

10. 生命会加重纯真的负担，但神秘却让灵魂学会飞翔。……阳光使人的眼睛发亮，却使小孩的眼睛和心灵同时发亮。难道是小孩离上帝更近，因为他们才刚刚向他道别？那样的亲近虽然恐怖，但它却正在消失。只要有了距离，我们才能更加舒适。

11. 谜语不是我的目的，我的诗探讨的是生命的本质。可是一个人不可能安全地面对一首诗，像面对准备好的晚餐，等着你的朋友到来一样。灵魂唱的歌是无法预期的。突然的火焰是神圣的危 险，开始与结束都是欢乐。

12. 我无法依循魏兹华斯先生的道路到天堂，我要依我自己艺术的道路到达。那是对我的召唤，和召唤他的声音一样真切，只是，召唤的来源会是一样的吗？我们只见过一次面，但我们的联系不是因为彼此相似的生命形态，而是对于灵魂淬炼的了解，灵魂的淬炼是由愤怒和拒斥而来的。

图书在版编目（CIP）数据

这世界，静默如初：狄金森经典诗选：全 2 册 /（美）狄金森著；王晋华译 .—北京：台海出版社，2017.7

ISBN 978-7-5168-1459-8

Ⅰ.①这… Ⅱ.①狄… ②王… Ⅲ.①诗集－美国－近代 Ⅳ.①I712.24

中国版本图书馆 CIP 数据核字（2017）第 149013 号

这世界，静默如初：狄金森经典诗选（下）

著　　者：［美］狄金森　　译　　者：王晋华

监　　制：薛　婷　　策划编辑：褚宇恒　　责任编辑：俞滟荣
版式设计：北京大观世纪文化传媒有限公司　　责任印制：蔡　旭

出版发行：台海出版社
地　　址：北京市东城区景山东街 20 号　　邮政编码：100009
电　　话：010-64041652（发行，邮购）
传　　真：010-84045799（总编室）
网　　址：www.taimeng.org.cn/thcbs/default.htm
E－mail：thcbs@126.com

经　　销：全国各地新华书店
印　　刷：北京瑞禾彩色印刷有限公司
本书如有破损、缺页、装订错误，请与本社联系调换

开　　本：880mm×1230mm　　1/32
字　　数：340 千字　　印　张：18.5
版　　次：2018 年 3 月第 1 版　　印　次：2018 年 3 月第 1 次印刷
书　　号：ISBN 978-7-5168-1459-8

定　　价：84. 00 元（全 2 册）